This is my dad.

He had a great idea to hatch lots of chicks from eggs.

EGGOMATIC

But before that could happen my little brother, Cheese (he's the one with the famous bottom), and his twin sister, Tomato, developed a strange problem . . .

Jeremy Strong once worked in a bakery, putting the jam into three thousand doughnuts every night. Now he puts the jam in stories instead, which he finds much more exciting. At the age of three, he fell out of a first-floor bedroom window and landed on his head. His mother says that this damaged him for the rest of his life and refuses to take any responsibility. He loves writing stories because he says it is 'the only time you alone have complete control and can make anything happen'. His ambition is to make you laugh (or at least snuffle). Jeremy Strong lives near Bath with his wife, Gillie, four cats and a flying cow.

This is the seventh book Jeremy Strong has written about Nicholas and his family.
The first six books, in reading order, are:

MY DAD'S GOT AN ALLIGATOR!
MY GRANNY'S GREAT ESCAPE
MY MUM'S GOING TO EXPLODE!
MY BROTHER'S FAMOUS BOTTOM
MY BROTHER'S FAMOUS BOTTOM GETS PINCHED!
MY BROTHER'S FAMOUS BOTTOM GOES CAMPING

Are you feeling silly enough to read more?

THE HUNDRED-MILE-AN-HOUR DOG
RETURN OF THE HUNDRED-MILE-AN-HOUR DOG
WANTED! THE HUNDRED-MILE-AN-HOUR DOG

JEREMY STRONG'S LAUGH-YOUR-SOCKS-OFF JOKE BOOK

Jeremy STRONG

My Brother's Hot Cross Bottom

Illustrated by Rowan Clifford

PUFFIN

PUFFIN BOOKS

Published by the Penguin Group
Penguin Books Ltd, 80 Strand, London WC2R 0RL, England
Penguin Group (USA) Inc., 375 Hudson Street, New York, New York 10014, USA
Penguin Group (Canada), 90 Eglinton Avenue East, Suite 700, Toronto, Ontario, Canada M4P 2Y3
(a division of Pearson Penguin Canada Inc.)
Penguin Ireland, 25 St Stephen's Green, Dublin 2, Ireland (a division of Penguin Books Ltd)
Penguin Group (Australia), 250 Camberwell Road, Camberwell, Victoria 3124, Australia
(a division of Pearson Australia Group Pty Ltd)
Penguin Books India Pvt Ltd, 11 Community Centre, Panchsheel Park, New Delhi – 110 017, India
Penguin Group (NZ), 67 Apollo Drive, Rosedale, North Shore 0632, New Zealand
(a division of Pearson New Zealand Ltd)
Penguin Books (South Africa) (Pty) Ltd, 24 Sturdee Avenue, Rosebank, Johannesburg 2196, South Africa

Penguin Books Ltd, Registered Offices: 80 Strand, London WC2R 0RL, England

puffinbooks.com

First published 2009
This edition produced for The Book People Ltd,
Hall Wood Avenue, Haydock, St Helens. WA11 9UL
001

Text copyright © Jeremy Strong, 2009
Illustrations copyright © Rowan Clifford, 2009
All rights reserved

The moral right of the author and illustrator has been asserted

Set in Baskerville
Made and printed in England by Clays Ltd, St Ives plc

British Library Cataloguing in Publication Data
A CIP catalogue record for this book is available from the British Library

ISBN: 978-0-141-34936-7

www.greenpenguin.co.uk

Penguin Books is committed to a sustainable
future for our business, our readers and our planet.
This book is made from Forest Stewardship
Council™ certified paper.

ALWAYS LEARNING   **PEARSON**

For chicken lovers of all ages

Contents

1. Inky Potatoes

'What on earth is it?' asked Mum, wrinkling her nose as she stared at the box. She always does that when she's puzzled by something and thinking hard. I don't see why wrinkling your nose helps. I've tried it at school when we have maths but it doesn't work.

Mum bent forward and peered at the big, plastic container. The bottom half was white, the top half clear. On the side was a dial and a switch. An electric plug hung off one corner like a bedraggled tail.

Dad stood there, hands on his hips, grinning with excitement. 'Isn't it great?'

'I don't know,' said Mum, 'because you haven't answered my question yet. What is it?'

'Have a guess,' Dad prompted.

Mum rolled her eyes and sighed. 'It's a box, Ron,' she said flatly. Dad's grin began to fade.

'Of course it's a box. Anyone can see it's a box, but what do you think it does?'

'It makes me cross,' Mum shot back. 'That's what it does.'

Dad's grin vanished. 'What do you mean? How can a box make you cross, for heaven's sake?'

'Because I don't know what it does, Ron, and I want you to tell me and stop asking me to guess when I haven't the faintest clue and if you don't tell me very, VERY soon I shall run away from home and join a circus. Anything for a quiet life.'

Dad looked at me helplessly. Mum wasn't going to play along with his little game so now he wanted me to have a go instead.

'Nicholas? What do you reckon?'

I shrugged. 'Think I'll join Mum at the circus.'

Dad turned to the twins, Cheese and Tomato. If you are wondering why my four-year-old brother and sister are called Cheese and Tomato it's because they were born in the back of a pizza delivery van.

They were! Our car broke down on the way to hospital and Mum climbed in the back of the pizza van. By the time she finally reached the hospital the twins had already been born. Their real names are James and Rebecca, but Dad thought it would be fun to call them Cheese and Tomato and the names have stuck.

Now Dad wanted the twins to guess what the box was. Cheese pulled the plug-in tail.

'Elephant,' he said, and Tomato jumped up and down with laughter. I could tell from her face that she was trying to think of something as silly as possible so as to outdo her brother.

'Sausage-car-bird!' she yelled, pulling her brother on to the floor, where they rolled about in hysterics, repeating their nonsense in as many ways as they could think of. 'Elephant-sausage!'

'Sock-bird-banana!'

At least that was an interesting change but Dad was not amused.

'Sometimes I wonder why I bother with you

lot. What's wrong with this family?'

'Their father, probably,' smiled Mum, smoothing Dad's hair with one hand, as if he were a small child. 'Tell us what it is, Ron,' she suggested. 'Then we can all get on with our lives.'

'You're no fun at all, any of you,' grumbled Dad. 'OK, it's an incubator.'

Now my nose really did wrinkle. 'A what-a-bator?'

'In-cu-ba-tor.'

'But what does it *do*, Dad?'

'Ah,' he began, and his excited grin came bouncing back. 'That's my brilliant idea, you see.

It's for chickens. It's a bit like a sunbed.'

'Since when have chickens needed a sunbed?' asked Mum. 'Do they want a suntan? Most of them are brown already. You'll have them strutting about the garden in dark glasses next.'

'I said it was LIKE a sunbed!' yelled Dad. 'And you don't put *chickens* in there, you dopey doodle, it's for their eggs.'

'Eggs need a suntan?' Mum asked, winding up Dad even more.

'NO! OF COURSE NOT! The box keeps the eggs warm until little fluffy yellow chicks hatch out, going cheep cheepy-cheep, and guess what? We shall have more egg-laying hens. Plus, it will be Easter in a few weeks and lots of people will see the chicks and they'll probably want some for themselves and I can sell off the ones we don't want. Now, am I brilliant or what?'

Mum was desperately pressing her lips together to stop herself bursting into giggles. 'I think you're probably more *what?* than brilliant.'

'Thank you for your support,' growled Dad. 'Huh, I go to all this trouble and you just make fun of me.'

Mum slipped an arm through Dad's. 'There, there. We all love you really,' she smiled. Dad grunted.

I guess I should explain that our back garden is like a mini-farm. We grow lots of vegetables and we now have eight chickens. The first five we got were the cockerel – he's called Captain Birdseye – and four hens, Mavis Moppet, Beaky, Leaky and Poop. Last month we got three new hens, Big Betty, Fusspot and Duvet (who is obviously VERY fluffy), but Poop has always been Cheese's favourite. Tomato loves her too because Poop likes to follow them everywhere.

'Inky-tater,' said Cheese. 'Poop can get a suntan.'

'No,' said Dad. 'You cannot put your pet chicken in here, Tomato. It's for eggs. And it's an incubator, not an inky potato.'

'Can Poop have sunglasses, Daddy?' Tomato pleaded. (She's got some big red ones that she loves.)

Dad groaned and eyed Mum. 'See what you've started?'

Mum smiled back at him. 'Well? Can Tomato's chicken have sunglasses?'

Dad stuck his fingers in his ears and started to sing. 'La-la-la, I can't hear anyone. La-la-la, you're all talking nonsense.'

La-la-la

I took the lid off the box and peered inside. A plastic foam lining covered several rows of heating elements. The lining had lots of egg-shaped hollows in it, enough for thirty eggs.

'Not all the eggs will hatch,' Dad explained. 'But we should have a pretty good success rate. I thought we could take the chicks down to the Easter Fair at your school, Nicholas. Children will love holding them and we can raise money for the new library.'

'Cool,' I said. 'I'll tell Mrs Morgan in class on Monday.'

'Now you're beginning to talk sense,' Mum admitted.

'I always talk sense,' said Dad. 'And don't raise your eyebrows at me like that and you can stop laughing. You too, Nicholas. I expect some support from my eldest son.' Then he strode off in a huff.

He won't be grumpy for long. My dad's not like that. He's always cracking jokes and being daft. He's a bit embarrassing at times but he's great!

2. What's Worse Than
Being Called Pants?

Guess what? We've got two new additions to the family! I don't mean Mum's suddenly given birth to another baby – it's something else. It started this morning when the doorbell rang.

It was Granny and her husband, Lancelot. I usually know when they're coming because they go roaring about on a monster motorbike wearing full leather gear. I mean Granny and Lancelot wear the leathers, not the motorbike! Lancelot recently bought himself a new jacket. It's got studs all over the back that spell out HELL'S DINOSAURS.

They must have come on one of their other bikes because I didn't hear them roar up and the windows didn't rattle either. It was Dad who answered the door.

'Oh, it's you,' he grunted.

'What a lovely, cheerful welcome from my favourite son,' Granny replied.

'I'm your *only* son,' Dad reminded Granny, giving her a dark look.

Lancelot chuckled. 'Hey, man! Who got out of bed on the wrong side this morning?' He flung an arm round Dad's shoulders. 'What's up, dude?' he asked. 'You're a bit down in the dumps.'

Dad sighed and told them about the incubator.

'It's for eggs,' Tomato butted in.

'We can make omelette,' added Cheese.

'That'd be a cheese omelette!' I suggested.

'Boom-boom!' said Dad, cheering up at once. 'That's my boy!'

Mum shook her head. 'Nicholas, you won't get *too* much like your father, will you?'

'He is going to be exactly like me,' declared Dad with pride.

'Oh dear,' chorused Granny and Mum, before looking at each other in surprise and laughing.

Dad didn't notice. He was staring at Lancelot's chest. His leather jacket seemed to have come alive. The whole chest area was heaving, as if an alien monster was about to burst out and attack us, like in one of those horror films.

'Got a problem with your stomach, Lancelot?' asked Dad.

'Oh! Yes. Almost forgot about them.' He

unzipped his jacket halfway, plunged in a big
hand and pulled out two black and white rabbits.

'Happy Easter!' he cried.

'But it's not Easter for four weeks,' I pointed
out.

'Couldn't wait that long. Had to get them
on the spot,' Lancelot explained, while Mum
cuddled one of the rabbits against her chest.

'They are so cute!' she said.

'Yum yum,' drooled Dad, patting his stomach.

'Ron! Don't be so horrible. They are not for eating!' Mum snapped at him.

'They're pets, man,' Lancelot explained, flicking his long, grey ponytail behind him. 'An early Easter present for each of the twins. We had to get them today because they were going cheap.'

'Going cheap?' I grinned. 'I thought chickens went cheep, not rabbits.'

'Boom-boom again!' cried Dad, punching the air.

Lancelot chuckled. 'You're on good form today, Nickers.'

Mum winced. 'Please don't call him that.'

'What? Nickers? Nickers doesn't mind, do you, mate?'

Well, actually, yes, I did mind. I mean, you wouldn't like it if you were called Pants, would you? Knickers is even worse. But Mum had already moved on to new problems and wanted to know if the rabbits would have babies.

Granny patted Mum's hand. 'They're both
males, so you won't have any problem with little
bunnies hopping about everywhere. You have
quite enough hopping about going on in your
house with those twins of yours.'

'Where are we supposed to keep them?' asked
Mum.

'In the oven,' muttered Dad and Mum
immediately dug her elbow into his side.

'Ow!'

'Just be sensible for a few moments, Ron, please. We are *not* going to keep them in the oven. They can go in the old chicken pen we used to have until you build them a proper hutch.'

Dad groaned. 'More work,' he grumbled.

I suddenly had a bright idea. 'Hey! There's going to be an Easter Rabbit Race at the school fair. We could enter these two.'

'Cool, dude,' Lancelot smiled. 'You could train them up. You know, give them some running exercises. There's a kid up our road who built an exercise machine for his dog. You could do the same. That'd be cool.'

Dad looked at Lancelot as if he was completely mad. (Takes one to know one – that's what I think!) 'I don't think that's a helpful suggestion, thank you very much,' he shot back.

Lancelot turned red. 'It was just an idea, man,' he shrugged and turned to Granny. 'Think it's time we went home, babe.' And off they went.

Dad says we are NOT going to have any rabbit exercise machines, thank you very much. 'Just chuck a few carrots for them to chase after,' he suggested.

So there we are. Not only are we growing vegetables in our garden, we are going to grow chickens now AND we have two rabbits to add to our backyard farm. (Not to mention a lot of carrots flying through the air!)

I wonder what our next-door neighbour Mr Tugg will say. He's already pretty annoyed that we have a goat, seven hens, a cockerel and a tortoise. I don't suppose he'll be the least bit pleased to discover that we're going to have a load more chicks, not to mention the rabbits, Saucepan and Nibblewibble.

Don't blame me! Those are the names the twins chose. (Don't forget Cheese calls his favourite hen Poop.) I tell you, everyone is bonkers in our house, except Mum and me. In fact sometimes I think we're the only sensible ones on the whole street.

3. Sticks and Stinkypoo Stuff

You'll never guess what! Our next-door neighbours, the Tuggs, have got a *child* staying with them! Amazing! They don't even *like* children! At least Mr Tugg doesn't.

Mrs Tugg is OK. She does aromatherapy and spends most of her time indoors. If you're wondering what aromatherapy is I can tell you because she did it on Rubbish, our goat, once. You don't normally give goats aromatherapy but Rubbish was in a bad way and we were grateful for any help. It worked too.

What you do is get loads of smelly stuff and people come to you and tell you their problems and you rub something gloopy on them and they go away happy. For example, suppose some woman goes to Mrs Tugg and says she's got a

bad foot? And not only that but she's also had a horrible letter from her bank and she's upset.

Mrs Tugg gets out some stinky stuff and rubs it on the woman's elbow, big toe, knee or wherever. She lights smelly candles and makes the woman sniff something with a weird name like Tping-Tpong or Rubber Bishop's Slipper. Then the woman pays Mrs Tugg lots of money and goes away feeling happier. And smelling rather odd.

Well, I think that's what happens. I could be wrong.

So Mrs Tugg is OK but Mr Tugg is PROBLEMO HUGE-O! He is like a volcano in full eruption and has a temper the size of Indonesia, which is where a lot of volcanoes come from. Also, he's definitely allergic to children. I know this because he always scowls at me as if I've done something awful. Mind you, Mr Tugg can't stand Dad either, so perhaps he just hates everyone.

But now there's a girl next door – a girl! She's nine, has long, straight, blonde hair and looks a bit like a doll. She's got big eyes and she's very clean and neat.

The first I knew about it was when I was out in the back garden checking the hens. (Lots of eggs today – Dad will be over the moon and jumping!) I was bending over to stroke Captain Birdseye – he's the cockerel – when something hit my back. I straightened up and just caught sight of this girl turning away from the fence.

'Hello!' I said and she swung back, looking surprised.

'Oh. Who are *you*?' she asked.

Honestly! The cheek of it! She spoke as if she'd lived next door all her life and *I* was the visitor.

'I'm Nicholas. I live here. Something just hit my back.'

'Really? Maybe it was that bird.'

'What bird?' I asked.

'It's gone now. I saw it fly over and it dropped

something. A bomb, maybe.'

I laughed and said it couldn't possibly be a bomb.

'It looked like a bomb. It might have been a stone. Or maybe an egg. Birds drop eggs sometimes. They steal them and drop them and eat them. I hate birds.' She gazed over the fence at the chickens. 'Chickens are birds,' she announced heavily, obviously including them on her list of Birds-She-Didn't-Like.

'They can't fly though, not properly,' I pointed out. She looked at me, opened her mouth, shut it and then asked if the stick had hurt me.

'I thought you said it was a stone,' I reminded her.

'Maybe it was. Maybe it wasn't. It could have been a carrot. You're always chucking carrots around over there.'

I explained about entering Saucepan and Nibblewibble in the Easter Rabbit Race and added that I couldn't possibly throw carrots at myself, could I?

'Well, it wasn't me. Do I look like a carrot-chucker?' She folded her arms stiffly and stared back at me, daring me to argue. Before I could say anything she launched into telling me who she was.

'My name's Cilla. My mum's in hospital for an operation. Aunty Gwen – she's not a real aunt but she said I could call her that – she says that when Mum comes out I can rub cactus oil on her and she'll feel a lot better.'

I guessed from the mention of cactus oil (I bet it's smelly) that Aunty Gwen was Mrs Tugg. 'What about your dad?' I asked.

'Stupid! Why should I rub cactus oil on him?'

'I meant, where *is* your dad?'

'He's working in another country, over the sea and far, far away,' Cilla delivered in a sing-song voice. 'So there's no one at home to look after me. I'm all on my own and I get very BORED.'

'Is that why you threw a stone at me?' I hinted.

'It wasn't a stone, it was a stick and I didn't throw anything. Look, you can see,' Cilla went on, waving her arms over the Tuggs' garden. 'There aren't any sticks *here* because it's neat and tidy. *Your* garden is a mess. No wonder you got hit by a stick. My uncle thinks your garden is a disgrace.'

'I know.'

'And he thinks your dad is a disgrace and you're a disgrace and your family must all be stupid because you give your children pizza names.'

I smiled at Cilla and she scowled back at me.

'I'm going indoors now,' she warned, 'and if a stick hits me I shall know who threw it because you're the only other person out here, so you'd better be careful, Mr Knicker-less.' And with that she disappeared back inside, slamming the door behind her. What a performance! Who did she think she was? Her Majesty, the Queen of Tuggland?

I can smell trouble brewing. At least, it's either trouble or Mrs Tugg is making up one of her stinkypoo creams.

4. Rabbit Eats Goat?

It's one thing after another! This morning there was the incident with Cilla from next door and this afternoon Saucepan and Nibblewibble escaped from the old chicken pen! (Dad's building a hutch and everything but it's not ready yet.) I know there are only two of them but they were everywhere. It was more like having ten rabbits whizzing round. They went zig-zagging and bouncing all over the place. I think they'll

have a good chance of winning the Rabbit Race if they're as speedy as that on the day!

Saucepan had managed to leap into the chicken run and seemed to think the hens were some kind of space hopper. He kept jumping on top of them for a ride and the poor hens were squawking like fury and scattering in every direction.

Meanwhile Nibblewibble was trying to bite Rubbish's ankles, which was brave but stupid and dangerous. Goats have a powerful kick and Rubbish could have scored a penalty with a single hoof-boot – using Nibblewibble as the football.

Fortunately the brain-dead goat hardly noticed.

Maybe Nibblewibble's teeth are blunt. Rubbish just stood there in the vegetable patch, calmly chewing Mum's cardigan. (Mum wasn't wearing it. Dad had put it on the scarecrow he'd built to frighten away any birds that fancied Brussels sprouts for dinner.)

It was Cheese and Tomato who told us about the escaped rabbits. Mum had sent the twins outside on a carrot-gathering exercise. Tomato came wandering back a little later to say that Saucepan was playing Bounce with the chickens and Nibblewibble was eating the Brussels sprouts that Mum and Dad were trying to grow. By the time we got outside the rabbit had given up on the sprouts and was attacking Rubbish instead. I half wish Nibblewibble had succeeded because it would have made an interesting newspaper headline.

RABBIT EATS GOAT!

Anyhow, Mum went shooting outside and found Cheese running round and round, chasing

after one or other or even both of the rabbits.
He was trying to catch them with a little fishing
net on a stick and having a great time, chuckling
away to himself.

'Oh no!' cried Mum. 'How on earth did those
rabbits escape?'

A spluttered snigger came from next door.
Cilla (yes – her again!) was peering over the fence
and watching our little circus performance. She

had a grandstand view. Round and round went Saucepan and Nibblewibble. Round and round went Cheese and Tomato. Round and round went Mum, and me too.

I don't know if you have ever tried to catch a running rabbit but I can tell you it's just about impossible. As soon as you grab them they squash themselves into the ground and wriggle out from beneath you. If you try scooping them up you quickly discover that their legs kick like crazy. Nibblewibble and Saucepan both appeared to have black belts in kung fu for rabbits.

I took off my jumper and hurled it over
Saucepan. He got tangled up and tripped over
himself. I grabbed hold of him and shoved him
back in the pen. Mum was still racing round
after Nibblewibble, with Cheese chasing after
her and Tomato close behind, pushing her
toy wheelbarrow at breakneck speed. (Tomato
usually gives Poop rides in it and obviously
thought the rabbits might like to go in it too.)

Nibblewibble headed
straight for me and I
stood there ready to
do battle, but he saw
me and did a U-turn,
straight into Mum's
waiting arms. A
moment later he'd been
shoved into rabbit-jail
alongside Saucepan.

By this time Cilla was
jumping up and down
and clapping her hands. Mum smiled. 'It's nice to
have children next door,' she said.

'There's only her,' I pointed out.

'She seems rather sweet, and very pretty,'
smiled Mum.

I kept quiet. Who would say Cilla was sweet?
After that business with the stick I didn't think so.
But Mum seemed to be quite taken with her. She
bent over the rabbit pen.

'I can't see any way they could have got out,' she said. She looked at Cheese and Tomato. 'Did either of you let the rabbits out?'

The twins smiled and nodded. So that solved that problem – almost.

'I told you not to,' groaned Mum in despair.

'Cilla said,' Tomato declared.

We all turned round and faced Cilla. I raised an eyebrow at her. She was definitely trouble with a capital T.

'Rabbits need to run around,' Cilla huffed,  folding her arms and fixing Mum with a stony glare. 'If rabbits don't get exercise they get VERY FAT and then they EXPLODE or they get stuck in their holes and starve. Either way they DIE and it will be YOUR fault.'

Mum was so gobsmacked that for a moment she couldn't think what to say. The twins filled in the silence.

'Don't want Nibblewibble to die,' whispered Tomato with a loud sniffle.

Mum shook her head. 'That was a very silly thing to say to small children,' she told Cilla before turning to the twins. 'The rabbits are *not* going to explode.' Mum rolled her eyes at me and muttered, 'If anyone is going to die it will be me from all that running about.' Unfortunately Cheese and Tomato heard her.

'DON'T DIE, MUMMY!' they yelled, rushing over and flinging their arms round both her legs.

Mum sighed heavily and gathered the twins in her arms. 'It's all right, darlings, nobody – no person and no rabbit – is going to die. We are all fine.' She looked across to Cilla, but unsurprisingly Cilla had vanished.

Mum took the twins inside while I calmed the hens down and collected Rubbish from the top of the compost bin. She'd wisely leaped up there for safety when we were all rushing about.

When I went back indoors I found Mum and the twins sitting round the kitchen table having a drink and cake so I joined in. Cheese and Tomato had quietened down a lot, probably because their mouths were stuffed full of chocolate cake.

'One piece only,' Mum told them.

'Big piece,' laughed Cheese. 'Really big, BIG, TYRANNO-NORMOUS piece!'

'Just eat what's on your plate, you little savage,' Mum chuckled before turning to me. 'I've been thinking, Nicholas. That girl next door, Cilla – I think we should invite her round for tea.'

I nearly choked on my cake. Invite Cilla round for tea? The stick-hurler who'd told the twins to let the rabbits out? The idiot-girl who'd said the rabbits would explode and sent the twins into hysterics? Even Mum had been upset by that, and now she was inviting Cilla into our HOUSE? Was my mum completely banana bonkerama?!

5. Meet Earthquake Woman!

I can't believe Mum invited that girl round! Mum seemed to think it would be nice for her to get to know us and maybe meet all our animals. I thought it was the worst idea ever.

Anyhow, you remember the incubator and Dad's plan to raise chickens? It's going pretty well. He's got about twenty eggs in there so far. Every morning before I go to school he checks the temperature and turns the eggs over so they get evenly warmed. He can't walk past the incubator without taking a little look.

'You're turning into a broody hen yourself,' Mum told him. 'I've often thought you walk in a funny way and now I know why. You're actually half chicken. It's the way you strut.'

Dad stared at her in silence, blinking rapidly. Mum's right! The hens blink the same way.

'It's the way you move your head too,' Mum went on. 'When you walk across the room your head lurches forward like a chicken's.' Mum waited for Dad's reaction. She didn't have to wait long.

He scraped at the floor slowly with one foot. He lifted one leg and took a step forward. His head stuck out. He tucked in his elbows and began to jerk them outwards as he walked. And then he began to talk – in chicken language.

'Praaarrrrk! Praaarrrkkk! PPPPPRRRAAARRKKK!' Suddenly Dad began to jerk wildly all over and he shuffled across to a chair. He squatted down, clucking frantically and going cross-eyed. At last he stopped and looked at us with a satisfied smile. 'Prrrrrk,' he murmured softly, getting up and looking back proudly at the chair seat. A single egg lay there.

I fell about while Mum wiped tears of laughter from the corners of her eyes.

'You are such a crazy clown!' she said.

'Prrraarrrkk!' Dad answered, strutting out of the room.

Anyhow, Dad reckons the eggs will take another couple of weeks before they start hatching. He says that when they are ready you can hear them cheeping *inside* the shell. I can't wait. And Dad says there'll be loads of chicks for the Easter Fair. It's all going to be brilliant!

Then, after school, Mrs Tugg brought Cilla round for tea. Lucky us!

'Poor little scrap,' I heard Mrs Tugg murmur to Mum. 'Her father's away on business and her mother's in hospital. She must miss them dreadfully. At least she can still go to her own school. It's not that far away.'

'How does she get on with your husband?'

Mum asked, and my ears pricked up because, like I said, Mr Tugg HATES children. (And animals and weeds and noise and laughter and untidiness and sunshine and happiness and I could go on but you'd get fed up.)

'Oh,' chuckled Mrs Tugg, 'he keeps right out of her way. You'd think she had measles. He spends most of his time hiding in the greenhouse, gently simmering. He'll probably boil over soon. You know what he's like. Sometimes I think there ought to be a way of using all that energy he puts into exploding. If only we could connect him to the National Grid he could provide half the town with electricity!' And she burst into more great, wobbly chuckles.

I like Mrs Tugg. She's kind, loves laughing and she's big. That means she wobbles quite a lot, like a tower block in an earthquake. That's actually quite funny because it means not only have we got Volcano Man living next door, but we also have Earthquake Woman! Mrs Tugg even likes our animals, which makes a nice change from her horrible husband.

Mrs Tugg went off home, leaving Cilla behind. At first Cilla simply stood in the kitchen doorway looking as if butter wouldn't melt in her mouth and playing with her long hair, the way girls do. They're always playing with their hair, or sucking it. Urgh!

She watched the twins and soon began nattering away with them as if they were her own brother and sister. Mum watched and smiled.

'She'll make a good mother,' Mum whispered to me.

'Mum, she's nine years old,' I reminded her.

'And you're thirteen. You can't expect her to be as grown up as you.'

'She's a maniac.'

'Don't be unkind, Nicholas. Give her a chance.'

'Have you forgotten what she did yesterday?' I asked in my most scathing voice.

Mum shook her head. 'Not at all, Nicholas.

That's why I've asked her round. Better the devil you know.' She raised her eyebrows cryptically and put a finger to her lips as Cilla drifted into the front room with the twins. They wanted to show her the 'inky-tater', as they continued to call it. Mum went off to sort some tea for everyone.

'The eggs go in there,' Tomato explained. She heaved her little shoulders and sighed deeply. 'And we have to wait months and weeks and years and a long, long, LONG-EVER-SO TIME and then a chicken pops out.'

'It must be a roast chicken by then,' Cilla said.

Tomato looked at Cilla in surprise and glanced across at me to see if I thought it would be a roast chicken too.

'Cilla is teasing you,' I told the twins. 'It won't be a roast chicken.'

Cilla studied the temperature dial on the front of the incubator. 'We could turn up the heat,' she suggested brightly. 'Then they'd all be roast chickens.'

'DON'T WANT ROAST CHICKENS!' wailed Cheese in a panic.

I glared at Cilla. 'She's teasing you again,' I explained. 'Just ignore her.'

Cilla grinned, squatted down and stared into

Cheese's face. 'It was a joke. You like jokes, don't you?'

Cheese's lower lip was sticking out like a plate, and trembling. He didn't like Cilla's kind of joke. But Cilla wasn't bothered and asked me how the incubator worked.

'Normally the hen sits on the eggs to keep them warm until they hatch. This way is simpler. The incubator keeps the eggs warm instead.'

'I bet the eggs would prefer to have hens sitting on them to keep them warm,' Cilla argued.

'Eggs can't think,' I pointed out.

Cilla pulled a sad face. 'If I were an egg I'd want to be under my mummy hen.'

'Your mum would have to be a humungously huge hen to get you underneath,' I growled. Cilla pulled a face at me and stuck out her tongue.

At that moment Mum called everyone for tea. She'd made little sandwiches and poured some fruit juice. Everything was all right until Cilla decided to help feed the twins. I used to do this,

but that was when they were small. Now Cilla
wanted to play at being mother, and she was
useless. Food quickly spread further and further
afield.

'They can feed themselves,' I snapped.
'They're not babies.'

'Goo goo, baby!' laughed Cheese, slopping
food on to the table. Cilla smirked. A beaker
got knocked over. The twins grew messier and
messier. Food spilled on to the floor but somehow

Cilla herself managed to remain perfectly clean and tidy.

'You *are* messy pups,' she declared, shaking her head.

'They don't normally make such a mess,' I scowled.

'Well, they have today,' replied Cilla with a wicked look in her eye. 'I'm afraid you've got such a lot of clearing up to do and it's time for me to go home now. Thank you for a lovely tea.

Goodbye. I'll see myself out.' And off she went, squashing spilled crumbs into the floor.

I followed her to make sure she'd gone. When I got back Mum was cleaning the table. 'Cilla has lovely manners. She's so polite and helpful too,' said Mum, tipping wodge-loads of crumbs into the dustpan. 'Look at the mess the twins have made – and Cilla's place is so tidy and clean as a whistle.'

I couldn't take any more. 'Mum, the table is a disaster zone because of the way Cilla fed Cheese and Tomato as if they were babies. There would have been a lot less mess if she'd left them alone. I'm sure she made them spill stuff deliberately,' I added darkly.

'Nicholas! Don't be so rude. And why on earth would she do that?'

'She probably thinks it's funny. In fact I think I shall call her Cilla the Spiller.' That cheered me up a bit but Mum didn't think it was funny.

'That's unkind. In fact I think Cilla should

come round more often. She's good company for the twins. It gives her something to do and keeps the twins out of my hair.'

Huh! So now my Mum's blind as well as bananas. Things are going from bad to worse.

6. One of Our Hens Is Missing

Cilla's been coming round for the last five days now. We've had a catalogue of disasters which I'm sure have mostly been her fault, but Mum either doesn't notice or she makes excuses for her:

Excuse Number One: 'She's just a bit clumsy.'
When Cilla appeared to trip in the kitchen and

 spilled half her drink down my trousers so it looked like I'd wet myself.

Excuse Number Two: 'She's not used to small children.' When she took Cheese

and Tomato upstairs
to the bathroom to
help them get clean
and managed to totally
soak them (and the
bathroom) with water.

Excuse Number Three:
'She's not used to
animals.' When she
tied up Rubbish right beside Mum's washing line
and the goat ate five pairs of pants,
three socks, and
munched a
gigantic hole in
my best football
shirt.

*Excuse Number
Four:* 'She's
not used to
vegetables.'
When Cilla

pulled up half of Dad's potato plants because she said the leaves were for making salad. She wondered why the leaves had little bobbles on the end.

'They're not bobbles,' complained Dad. 'They're teeny tiny potatoes that won't be able to grow now because you've ripped them out of the ground.'

'You sound just like Mr Tugg,' Cilla answered with a sweet smile and wide eyes, leaving Dad spluttering with rage and even more like Mr Volcano next door.

'She's only nine,' said Mum. 'Leave the poor girl alone.'

Am I the only one who can see that Trouble follows Cilla wherever she goes? I can't understand why Mum is so keen on the little brat. I think Dad is beginning to agree with me though.

We haven't only had disasters either. There's a mystery too – a chicken and egg mystery.

Dad reckons he had at least twenty eggs in the incubator but now there are only fourteen. Mum said he must have counted wrong.

'I didn't,' Dad protested. 'There were twenty, at least. I remember because I had to use all the fingers on both hands, twice.'

'Eggs don't simply vanish, Ron,' Mum said. 'Unless of course the little baby chicks stick their legs out of the bottom and run off.' She started giggling.

'Not funny,' Dad muttered. Mum lifted her arm and made two fingers run up it, like an escaping egg.

'Oh that is hilarious, I don't think,' Dad snapped. Cheese and Tomato started to tug at Dad's leg and he looked down at them crossly. 'Now what?'

'Poop has gone,' said Cheese.

'What do you mean, she's gone? Gone where?'

Tomato heaved her shoulders in a big shrug and let them drop. 'We can't find her.'

'Where have you looked?' asked Dad.

Tomato spread out the fingers on one hand and began counting them off. 'In the garden, in the shed, in the rabbit hutch, in the kitchen, in the toilet –'

'The toilet?' interrupted Dad. 'Why on earth would she be in there?'

Cheese gave him a pale smile. 'Don't be silly, Daddy – to do a poop, of course.'

'Oh. Why didn't I think of that?' said Dad, shaking his head. 'Well, we'd better all go on a Poop search, hadn't we? I expect we'll find her in the garden with the other hens, safe and sound.'

Dad took Tomato's hand, Cheese held on to me and we all set off on a hen hunt, starting with the chicken run. There was Captain Birdseye, strutting his stuff in front of Mavis Moppet, Beaky and Leaky, Big Betty and Fusspot. We found Duvet asleep in the hen house, but there was no sign of the twins' favourite, Poop. We searched everywhere. We checked the rabbits, but they were safe in the new hutch. Meanwhile

Tomato followed us round murmuring, 'I've already looked there,' every time we peered into, over or under anything.

'What are you doing?' Cilla called from next door.

'Poop is missing,' Mum told her.

'Maybe she ran away,' Cilla answered.

'Hens don't run away,' I told her. 'So maybe she didn't.'

'I know a cat that ran away,' Cilla said. 'It didn't like its owner,' she continued, fixing me with one of her glares. 'So it ran away to find someone nice and kind who would look after it properly and guess what?'

'What?'

'IT NEVER CAME BACK.' Cilla grinned at me triumphantly. I'd fallen right into her little trap. Rats!

'DON'T WANT POOP TO RUN AWAY!' squeaked Cheese, clutching Mum's leg in his panic.

'It's all right, darling. Cilla was joking, weren't you?' Mum added, looking at little angel face from next door.

I was trying to think of something sharp and clever to say to Cilla when several tons of molten lava came spilling out of next door in the shape of Mr Tugg. He was holding something brown, scruffy and flappy at arm's length. It was, of course, Poop.

'I'm fed up with your blasted animals invading my home!' he yelled, and his face got redder and redder, until it looked like a gigantic tomato. 'Last month it was that wretched goat of yours, and now it's this nasty flappy thing.'

'It's only a hen,' Dad began.

'Only a hen!' repeated Mr Tugg in amazement. 'ONLY A HEN? I'm not running a farm! I have a nice, clean, normal house and now we've got bits of straw all over the place and chicken poo from here to kingdom come. Do you allow hens to wander about your house?'

'Poop often comes indoors, Mr Tugg,' Mum told him. 'She's the twins' special favourite hen and likes to follow them everywhere.'

Mr Tugg's eyes were bulging with disbelief and he started to boil. 'You-you-you ALLOW a HEN into your HOUSE?!' he spluttered.

A twinkle came into Dad's eyes. 'Indeed we do, Mr Tugg. It makes our egg deliveries so much easier. We train all our hens to come into

the kitchen
and lay
their eggs
straight
into a
saucepan
or a frying
pan, ready for
cooking.'

'I've had enough of your
nonsense,' steamed Mr Tugg,
dropping Poop over the fence and
into our garden. The hen scrabbled
quickly across to Tomato and into her arms.

In the meantime Mr Tugg started up again
about preventing hens from coming anywhere
near his garden, let alone his house.

'I'm sorry,' said Mum, 'but I have no idea how
one of our hens got into your house in the first
place, Mr Tugg. Their wings are clipped so they
can't fly over the fence.'

'Exactly,' added Dad. 'You didn't lend them your front-door key, did you?'

'Of course I didn't!' bellowed Mr Tugg as he rapidly reached tomato colour once more.

'Maybe they dug a tunnel,' Dad suggested. 'I couldn't find my spade this morning. I bet they pinched it. Those chickens are always nicking my tools.'

Mum hastily brought things back to a more sensible level. 'As you can see, the hens are also shut in their run and can't get out unless someone takes them out.'

'Your twins,' hinted Mr Tugg.

'Not necessarily,' I murmured, staring across at Mr Tugg's house. There was a face at a bedroom window. It was Cilla. Everyone turned to see what I was looking at.

'Cilla's been indoors all morning,' said Mr Tugg loftily and he turned his back on us and headed back inside.

I was about to point out that Cilla had been in

the garden earlier but Dad spoke first.

'In that case it's a mystery we shall never solve, isn't it?' Dad called after the disappearing figure, and we went indoors. I bet I know who took Poop into the Tuggs' house, and I bet Dad does too. (Can't trust Mum to see the truth of anything that goes on with Cilla at the moment. Huh.)

As for the missing eggs, we still don't know what's going on there. Dad says he reckons Mr Tugg is creeping into our house when nobody is looking and secretly stealing our eggs.

'Why would he do that?' I asked.

'Because he's not of this planet, that's why,' hissed Dad. 'He comes from Mars. I've been telling you that since you were born. And everyone knows that Martians are stark staring stonking bonkers!'

7. The Curse of the Phantom Scarecrow

Mum's been moaning about finding bits of straw all over the house. 'It gets everywhere. You lot must walk it in from the garden on the bottom of your shoes.'

'We've never had a straw problem before,' Dad pointed out.

Mum examined her shoes. 'It's up the stairs. It's in the bathroom. It's in the front room, the kitchen, the bedrooms – wisps of straw all over the place.'

Dad pulled at his beard thoughtfully and narrowed his eyes. 'Hmmm. That sounds like the Curse of the Phantom Scarecrow to me. Have you considered that possibility?'

Mum did the same narrowing of the eyes

and gazed straight back at him. 'And have you considered the possibility that you are as daft as a haystack?' she asked.

'That must be where all the straw comes from!' I grinned. 'It's not the Curse of the Phantom Scarecrow – it's Dad being a haystack!'

'Boom-boom!' cried Dad and he saluted me.

Mum folded her arms. 'Nevertheless,' she began, 'you two are going to clean the house of every wisp of straw because I am fed up with doing it myself. I shall go outside now and have a chat with the hens. At least they talk sense.'

I smiled at them both. I love it when we argue like that. My dad is always coming up with crazy ideas and suggestions, and it doesn't take much to wind up my mum.

Anyhow, it was true about the straw. It *was* getting annoying, and I helped Dad clean it up. He was still pretty puzzled about the missing eggs though, and we talked about it during the big straw clean-up. Apparently several more eggs had vanished. I said that Mum may have taken some for cooking but Dad shook his head.

'It's more mysterious than that,' he said and started muttering about aliens in UFOs and a possible egg shortage on Planet Zogg. However, his mind was soon taken off that little problem by something equally strange: my little brother Cheese's bottom.

What you may not know is that my brother has got one of the most famous bottoms in the country. It's true. It's been on television! I mean his actual bottom has been seen on TV!

When the twins were about eighteen months old, Cheese got involved in a TV advert for disposable nappies called Dumpers. You may have seen the ad yourself, with Cheese crawling around wearing one of the nappies. When they were making the ad Cheese escaped and managed to crawl his way on to the *Six o'Clock News* by mistake. The thing was, he wasn't wearing his nappy. In fact he was hardly wearing anything at all, so millions of viewers got a bit of a shock and Cheese became an overnight sensation!

Cheese's bum has been famous ever since, and now he had a problem with it. It was itchy, sore and uncomfortable.

'It's very red,' said Mum. 'I'll put some cream on it.'

'Double or single?' joked Dad.

'Don't mock. It's obviously very uncomfortable for the poor chap. I don't know what all those little red dots are. It's as if his bottom's been pricked with something.'

'Perhaps he sat on a hedgehog,' Dad suggested. Mum ignored him.

'If it doesn't improve quickly I shall take him to the doctor. There, does that feel any better?' she asked Cheese. My brother looked a bit unsure but he toddled off to find his sister.

'Strange,' murmured Mum, watching him go. 'I wonder if he's allergic to the new rabbits?'

'RABBITS PUT SPOTS ON BOTTS,' Dad said brightly. 'That'd make a good headline.'

'FUNNY BUNNY MAKES BOTTY

SPOTTY,' I suggested and we both rolled about.

Then, this afternoon, guess what? Tomato had exactly the same thing! Dad was in the middle of toasting some hot cross buns for everyone when we heard wailing from upstairs. Dad looked at me and rolled his eyes heavenwards.

'Your mother's probably broken a fingernail,' he grunted. 'Quick, call an ambulance!'

'Dad! That's Cheese, or Tomato,' I said.

'Boo! I'm here!' cried Cheese from beneath the table, popping his head out.

'Definitely Tomato,' I nodded. 'I wonder what's up.'

We found out a minute later when Mum came in, carrying Tomato, bare from the waist down and sporting a rather red bottom. Mum stroked Tomato's hair.

'It's the same as Cheese's,' she said. 'I can't think what's causing it. It's such an angry-looking rash.'

Dad put a plate load of buns on the table and

smiled. 'I think I'd call that a hot cross bottom.'

I shook my head and grinned. 'It's not a hot cross bottom, Dad. It's a hot cross bum!'

'Boom-boom!' shouted Dad. 'Give the boy a coconut!' He began singing loudly, and it was such a brilliant song that we instantly joined in, even the twins. Dad grabbed a saucepan from the kitchen counter and started banging it with a wooden spoon, like a drum.

We went prancing round the kitchen, and out into the garden, with Dad leading the way, banging on the pot. Mum was jiggling Tomato

up and down in her arms and I put Cheese in
the little barrow and wheeled him along. Even
Nibblewibble, Saucepan and Poop joined in.
Down the garden we went, singing at the tops of
our voices.

'Hot cross BUMS! Hot cross BUMS! One a
penny, two a penny, hot cross BUMS!'

Mr Tugg came out of his house and stared at
us, his jaw hanging from the bottom of his face in
disbelief. Cilla came rushing out too and leaned
over the fence. She couldn't take her eyes off us.
She couldn't help smiling either. In fact I thought
she was going to burst out laughing, which would
have made a change. I think she was actually
dying to join in. She's weird.

'Come on, Cilla,' shouted Dad. 'Why don't you
come over and join in the fun?'

Before she could answer, Mr Tugg went rather
red and said that he wasn't going to put up with
our nonsense. He took Cilla by the hand and
marched back indoors, with Cilla looking over

her shoulder at us and smirking. For once it looked like a real smile!

If I didn't know better I'd think Cilla the Spiller secretly wanted to prance round the garden with us and sing along. But she doesn't know how to join in — she only knows how to *start* mayhem. I just can't make her out.

8. Spotty Botties

What is it with all this straw? Dad and I only
went round the house yesterday doing a thorough
clean and now it's back. There's more straw
in our house than there is in the chicken coop!
I discovered some floating in the toilet this
morning. How did it get there? Dad said maybe
the Phantom Scarecrow has been using our loo!

We even had Rubbish in the
house. She was following
the trail, chewing on little
wisps, and had
wandered in as
far as the bottom
of the stairs. I
found her with
her front legs

on the second step and a mouth stuffed full of stalks. Thankfully I spotted her and took her outside, otherwise I think we would have had a hot cross mum!

The twins' bottoms aren't getting any better either. Mum asked Mrs Tugg to come round this morning and take a look. I think Mum was hoping she might have some magic cream that would solve the problem, but she simply shook her head when she saw the pair of spotty botties.

'I've never seen anything quite like that,' declared Mrs Tugg.

'What do you think has made those little red prick marks?' asked Mum.

'I've no idea. I can give you some camomile cream but I expect you've tried that already?' asked Mrs Tugg, and Mum nodded.

'I shall ring Nicholas's gran and see if she has any suggestions. If it doesn't improve soon I'll have to take them to the doctor and let her have a look,' Mum decided.

So after school, Granny and Lancelot came zooming round on one of their motorbikes. Poor Cheese and Tomato. They had to lie there and have their bottoms inspected by the whole family. We all stood there, looking at the uncomfortable rash, with Dad and Lancelot pretending to be VERY IMPORTANT AND CLEVER doctors. They stroked their chins and spoke to each other in silly voices.

'Hmmm. Very strange. What do you think, Doctor Finkletinkle?' asked Lancelot.

'I think when botts have spots and there are lots of spots, we have no idea, Doctor Potts,' replied Dad, and they both chuckled to themselves.

Anyhow, Granny had no idea what was causing the rash and they went roaring back home on their bike while I went to help Dad turn the eggs in the incubator. He was gazing at the little machine and scratching his head.

'All the eggs are there,' he murmured. 'I don't understand it.'

'Maybe you counted them wrongly yesterday?' I suggested.

'I'm not an idiot, Nick. I know I look like an idiot and talk and behave like an idiot but I'm not one really. I do know how to count eggs.' He sighed. 'Oh well, at least all the eggs are back. That's the important thing. They should start hatching any day now.'

Dad and I bent our heads over the incubator but there was still no sound of cheeping.

I went out to the garden and found Cilla staring over our fence, bored out of her mind as usual. She didn't even answer when I called 'hello' to her. I almost feel sorry for her. (I said 'almost' – I didn't say I *did*.) It wouldn't be much fun living with Mr Tugg. She kicked something with her foot, picked it up and looked at me to see if I was watching. It was a large rock, which she carried across Mr Tugg's wonderfully green lawn and put down, right in the middle. She scowled at me and came back to the fence.

I should tell you that Mr Tugg spends HOURS AND HOURS working on his lawn. I have seen him go down on his knees, measure the length of grass blades with a ruler and trim them with little scissors until the lawn is perfect.

'I don't think Mr Tugg will be very happy when his lawnmower goes over that stone,' I told Cilla. She threw me a faint smile.

'Oh dear,' she answered flatly. It was as if she was deliberately looking for trouble, which meant I didn't want to be anywhere near her!

Anyhow, I had to milk Rubbish, which is a job and a half, I can tell you. I set the milk pail between her legs but the daft goat likes to shuffle about while she's being milked. If you're not careful, before you know it, she's stuck one foot in

the bucket, or kicked it over and spilled the lot.

'Rubbish is a stupid name for a goat,' Cilla called out.

'Yeah? Can you think of a better one?'

Cilla shrugged and thought, while I pulled away beneath the goat and milk spurted into the pail.

'Dennis,' she said eventually.

'You can't call a she-goat Dennis!' I said.

'You can't call her Rubbish either,' Cilla answered. 'All right, Harriet. There's a girl at my school called Harriet and she looks like a goat. She's got long floppy ears and she smells. Why did you call her Rubbish anyway?'

'Because she eats rubbish and she's pretty much rubbish at doing anything.' There was a clatter as the goat stuck one foot in the bucket. I quickly yanked it back out. 'See what I mean?'

'She's funny,' said Cilla, cheering up a fraction. There was a long silence while I carried on milking and then Cilla spoke up again. 'I like your house. And your garden.' She took a quick squint round the Tuggs' neat lawn and flower beds. 'This garden is B-O-R-R-I-N-G-E.'

'Borringe?' I repeated. 'Their garden is borringe?'

'NO, STUPID!' shouted Cilla. 'BORING!'

'Oh!' I smiled and didn't bother to correct her because she was obviously on a short fuse, which was hardly surprising. Anyone who lived with Mr Tugg would be driven bonkers eventually. I guessed that must be what Cilla's problem was. She was just bored and fed up with being on her own with Mr and Mrs Tugg. I don't suppose it was much fun, especially with a crazy family like mine next door.

Cilla frowned and scratched herself. 'Can I come round later?'

I groaned inwardly. 'I expect so. You'll have to check with my mum when she gets back from the Health Centre.' I explained about the twins' little problem. Cilla nodded.

'That's why you were singing that song yesterday,' she said. 'Anyway, see you later.' She'd obviously cheered up a bit because she went skipping back indoors and I could hear her singing to herself. 'Hot cross bums! Hot cross bums!'

Mr Tugg was probably out, or she wouldn't have dared.

A bit later on both Cilla and Mrs Tugg came round. Cheese and Tomato pounced on Cilla with delight and quickly vanished upstairs, while Mrs Tugg whispered in Mum's ear and soon the two of them had moved into the kitchen and shut the door. Something secret was being discussed and Dad and I could only guess at what it might be.

'I think Mr Tugg has run away with another woman,' Dad muttered, waggling his eyebrows at me.

'Dad!' I was embarrassed. Besides, it was a daft suggestion. Who'd want to go out with Mr Tugg?

Well, I suppose Mrs Tugg did, once upon a time. But that must have been donkey's years ago, when Mr Tugg was young, and had more hair, and was thinner, and possibly less angry. I turned to Dad.

'I think Mrs Tugg secretly likes our farm animals but she doesn't dare tell Mr Tugg in case he explodes. So she wants to come round here and play with them. Maybe she could train Saucepan and Nibblewibble for the Easter

Rabbit Race,' I suggested.

Dad shook his head. 'No, I don't think that's it. Why would she go into the kitchen with your mother and start whispering? It's something more serious.' Dad suddenly grinned from ear to ear. 'I know! Mr Tugg has a spotty botty!'

'Dad!'

He nodded at me happily. 'I bet you that's what it is.'

Cilla and the twins came thundering down the stairs, looked at us briefly as if to check we were still there, and hurried into the front room, shutting the door behind them. I was going to peep in to see what they were up to but at that moment the kitchen door opened and Mrs Tugg came out. She gave us a pale smile, murmured 'goodbye' and went back next door.

Mum came out of the kitchen and turned to us with a smile. 'Well,' she began. 'Guess what? Cilla's got a hot cross bottom too!'

Dad gave me a satisfied smile. 'I was pretty

close,' he declared.

I gave Dad a weak smile. Secretly I was hoping I wasn't going to be the next victim of the Hot Cross Bum bug.

9. Going Cheep!

It's been a banana bonkers day today! I wish
you'd been here to see it. First of all there was the
straw.

Yesterday evening, after Cheese and Tomato
had had their backsides smeared with anti-itch
cream and put to bed, Mum, Dad and I went
through the house from top to bottom with the
vacuum cleaner, a dustpan and brush and a big

plastic sack. Then we set off on a straw hunt.
We gathered up every single bit of straw we
could find, took it all outside and dumped it back
in the hen coop.

So, what was the first thing I saw when I got up
this morning? You guessed! Bits of straw all over
my bedroom floor. What's going on? There was
practically enough straw on my floor to build a
thatched roof over my bed!

Then there were the eggs. Half of them were
missing again. Dad was tearing out his hair. If

this goes on much longer he'll end up as bald as Mr Tugg.

'I don't understand,' he wailed, over and over. 'What's happening to them?'

Before we could do anything about it a miserable Tomato wandered in, complaining that she was still hot and itchy.

'I've had enough of this,' muttered Mum, sweeping Tomato into her arms. 'I'm taking the pair of them back to the Health Centre. It must be those wretched rabbits that Granny and Lancelot brought. I bet they've got rabbit fleas or something. The rabbits are the only new thing that's come to this house in the last few days.'

'Apart from Cilla,' I added.

Mum gave me a steady look. 'I suppose that's a joke, Nicholas. Cilla is hardly likely to bring fleas into the house. Give her a break – she's lonely and miserable and needs a bit of cheering up. You two get rid of this straw while I take the twins to the doctor.'

While Mum did that, Dad and I had another clean up. I had almost finished in my bedroom when I heard a faint, high-pitched squeaky noise coming from somewhere behind me.

I looked round but couldn't see anything. Then I heard it again. It seemed to be coming from beneath my bed. I was about to get down on my hands and knees to take a look when a tiny, yellow, wobbly bundle of fluff came staggering out from beneath the bed. The little chick looked at me, opened its beak and said *cheep*! Just like chicks do.

I think it was asking for directions, like *where am I?* Or *can you tell me where my mum is, please?*

I hurried to the stairs and yelled down. 'Dad! You'd better take a look at this.'

Dad came thundering up, two at a time and then stood there with his eyes popping while the little chick went on adventures round his feet, pecking at his shoelaces as if they were worms.

'Where did that come from?' Dad squeaked in a voice almost as high as the chick's.

I shrugged. 'My guess would be an egg.'

'Very funny,' grunted Dad in a more normal tone. 'Of course it does. I mean – what is it doing up here?'

'It was under my bed.'

'What was it doing under there?' asked Dad in exasperation.

'Looking for a pair of socks? I don't know, Dad. It just came wandering out, as if it had been there for ages, lurking.'

We were about to look beneath my bed when

Dad suddenly grabbed my arm and froze.

'What?' I asked, but Dad put a finger to his lips. We waited a moment, and then I heard it too. *Cheep cheep cheep.* We looked at the chick at our feet. He (I've decided it was probably male because it had such big feet) had his head cocked on one side. *He was listening too!*

'There's another one,' Dad whispered. 'In one of the other bedrooms!'

'Why are we whispering?' I whispered back.

'I don't know,' answered Dad, in a whisper.

'Are you scared?' I asked him.

Dad looked at me scornfully and spoke in a proper voice at last. 'Of course I'm not scared. I was surprised, that's all. Come on, we'd better find where it is.'

We went out to the landing and there was the second chick waddling along towards the top of the stairs, as if it was on its way out.

'That's two chicks, Dad. They must have come from the incubator.'

'Impossible. The incubator is downstairs and it's got a lid on it.'

At that moment another chick came waddling out of Mum and Dad's bedroom. Dad almost exploded with confusion.

'What's going on?' he yelled.

And that was when a pair of chicks came running from Cheese and Tomato's room, chirping like mad, closely followed by another one from my room and two from Mum and Dad's.

'Aaaaaargh!' yelled Dad, as he was quickly

surrounded by a chirping, cheeping,
bouncing, scrabbling, pecking mass
of little yellow pom-poms on legs.

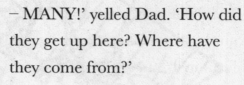

'They are so
cute!' I grinned.

'They are so
– MANY!' yelled Dad. 'How did
they get up here? Where have
they come from?'

    I went back to my room,
where I found another chick in
the process of emerging from
beneath my bed. I lay down on
the floor and peered underneath.
I could see a strange lumpy shape
in the darkness, so I reached in and pulled it out.
It was a nest.

'Take a look at this, Dad,'
I shouted out. He shuffled in
nervously, worried about stepping
on more runaway chicks.

We stared at the nest. Basically it was an old shoe box, stuffed with straw. Inside were several bits of broken eggshell, plus one unhatched egg.

Dad turned to me.

'Nicholas, why have you got a chicken nest under your bed?'

'No idea,' I answered truthfully.

'That nest was not made by a chicken,' Dad

pointed out and I agreed.

'No, it wasn't.'

'So who made it?' asked Dad.

We heard the front door open as Mum returned with the twins. 'You'll never guess what the doctor – EEK! RON! NICHOLAS! The house is full of chickens, I mean chicklets, chicks, you know, small ones, baby ones! Quick! Help me! They're all over the place!'

Dad grabbed my shoulders. 'OK, son, this is an emergency. We need a plan. You . . . um, you . . . um, and I'll . . . um, you-I'll-your mother . . . um, we'll –'

'Dad!' I interrupted. 'Go and help Mum. I'll sort out things up here.'

'Right!' said Dad, and he hurtled downstairs, two, three, four at a time. In fact I think he fell the last six, judging by the noise he made. It sounded like ten large wardrobes doing somersaults, and not succeeding.

To cut a long story short it took us half an hour

to round up all the chicks. There were eleven
altogether, all yellow, all fluffy and all TOTALLY
adorable. While that was going on Mum told us
what had happened at the Health Centre and
slowly the chick puzzle was solved.

'The doctor said the rash was probably caused
by something like straw,' said Mum.

'Straw?' repeated Dad, stroking his beard and
trying to look wise. (Which in Dad's case is VERY
DIFFICULT!)

Mum nodded. 'I asked the twins if they'd
been playing with straw or sitting on straw and
they went very quiet. I took that as a *yes*. I asked
a few more questions and discovered that they
have been playing a game of pretending to be

hens hatching out chicks. They made little nests, hidden away all over the house. They packed them with straw, put eggs inside and then sat on them to hatch them out.'

Dad stopped stroking his beard and sat up straight. 'I see. Do you think they both might be as mad as a fish with an umbrella?'

Mum laughed. 'No. Not mad. It was a game and they were only doing what they were told to do.'

My eyes popped. 'Someone TOLD them to make nests and sit on the eggs?'

'Exactly,' Mum answered.

'But who?' demanded Dad.

At that moment we heard a massive, ginormous explosion from next door.

'CILLA!'

Mr Tugg was in full eruption! We hurried out into the back garden to see what was going on.

10. The Mystery Is Solved

Mr Tugg came bursting out of his back door like a straw tornado. He appeared to be fighting some kind of monster but all we could actually see was straw whirling around him. He was closely followed by Mrs Tugg, wobbling wildly and giving little shrieks of dismay. Behind Mrs Tugg came a stream of little chicks. And after that lot came Cilla, scratching herself again and looking rather pleased.

We gathered at the fence to watch Mr Tugg doing his war dance. I've seen this a few times now. He does it about once a month. There's always something that pops up and annoys him so much he has to express himself like this. It goes in stages:

Stage One: Mr Tugg hurries round the garden

shouting to himself and waving his fists at the sky.

Stage Two: Mr Tugg reaches the centre of the garden, where he stops. By this time he has run out of words and can only grunt, snort, stamp his feet, yell, clench his hands, howl and generally pull sixteen different horrible faces in quick succession and then – repeat, several times.

Stage Three: Mr Tugg is now purple and goes into meltdown. He falls silent, but you know he's just building up for the final eruption. He looks up at the sky. He raises his arms. His body trembles and at last he grits his teeth and ROARS!

'AAAAAAARRRRRGGGGGGGHHHH!!!'

Poor Mr Tugg. Nobody does a volcano impression quite like him. We all waited until it was over. Mum had slipped into the kitchen while this was going on. Now she reappeared with a tray and two mugs.

'Cup of tea, Mr Tugg? Mrs Tugg?'

Mrs Tugg took the tray gratefully and handed her husband a mug. Now that he'd let off steam, Mr Tugg was quieter, though still rather fizzy.

'That girl's been making nests under the beds,' stuttered Mr Tugg. 'With YOUR eggs,' he added accusingly, looking straight at my dad.

'Oh dear,' said Dad, sounding a wee bit like Cilla when I'd spoken to her about the stone on the lawn.

We all turned to Cilla, who frowned back. 'Eggs need someone to look after them,' she stated. 'You shouldn't put them in an incubator. They need a mummy. I was hatching them out myself. Anyway, we put them back afterwards.'

'It's a wonder you didn't break any, sitting on them like that,' said Mum.

'Huh! I'm not stupid,' Cilla grunted.

'Hmmm, that's a matter of opinion,' sighed Dad.

Mr Tugg waggled a finger at Cilla. 'She's not from here,' he declared. 'She comes from Mars. She's an alien. She can't possibly be human. She put a rock in the middle of my lawn yesterday. A rock! On my lawn! Can you believe that?'

'I was bored.' Cilla did her arm-folding exercise. 'Your house is the most boring house in the history of boring houses. You won't let me do anything. There's no one to play with. The only fun I have is when I go next door to *their* house and look after Cheese and Tomato.'

I was beginning to understand how Cilla felt. For a few moments there was a stunned silence because nobody could argue with what she had just said, except possibly Mr Tugg. He looked at the rest of us. Maybe he was waiting for us to rush to his defence. He'd have to wait a long time.

Mr Tugg took a deep breath and drew himself up to his full height – which was not very tall. He was obviously going to say something important. 'My house is full of straw,' he hissed. (Not *that* important, then.)

'So is ours,' Mum pointed out.

'Chickens have pooped on my carpets,' added Mr Tugg.

'Ours too,' Mum agreed.

'One of your chicks ate my breakfast!' snapped Mr Tugg.

Dad shrugged. 'Huh! One of my chicks *was* my breakfast,' he declared.

'Dad!' I was aghast. 'You never!'

'Just joking,' Dad grinned.

'Your dad's funny,' giggled
Cilla.

This was exactly the sort
of remark to make Mr Tugg
even crosser. 'Do I take it
that you're not going to do
anything about any of this?' he stormed.

'Yes,' said Dad, putting on
a childlike voice and wringing
his hands. 'Please can I have
my chicks back?'

'WHO'S GOING TO
CLEAN MY HOUSE?' Mr
Tugg bellowed.

Mum stepped forward. 'Mr Tugg, it was Cilla
who caused all this. Cilla
lives with you, not us. None
of this was our idea, but
we're not going to lose sleep
over it. Perhaps if you'd

found something fun for Cilla to do none of this would have happened. As it is, she's come round to our house almost every day and helped the twins build nests everywhere.'

Phew! My mum's so brave! She was staring straight at an erupting volcano and telling it off! She's amazing, and she hadn't finished either.

'We have a house to clean too and we're going to get on with it. Oh, before you return your dirty mug perhaps you could wash it up for us?'

And we went back indoors. I don't know how long Mr Tugg stayed out there fuming, but Mrs Tugg came round to see us a short while ago. Apparently Mr Tugg is saying Cilla can't stay there any longer.

'I don't know what to do,' wailed Mrs Tugg. 'Cilla's not a bad girl, she's just —'

'Wicked?' suggested Dad.

'Ron!' Mum glared at him. 'Poor girl. I feel very sorry for her. Where will she go?'

'That's the problem,' Mrs Tugg explained.

'Her mother doesn't come out of hospital for a week yet, and her father's not home for another month, but I'm afraid my husband won't have her in the house.'

At that moment I think my brain must have gone on holiday to somewhere very far away, like another planet, or even another universe, because I opened my mouth and I heard myself say something really, REALLY unexpected.

'Maybe she could stay here.'

'WHAT!?' Dad's eyes were practically popping out of his head, but Mum threw an arm round me and hugged me, hard.

'Nicholas, what a wonderful idea. I'm so proud of you,' she said happily.

Dad was shaking his head. 'I'll never understand this family,' he grunted. 'Cilla has just created mayhem in two homes and now you're inviting her to stay?'

'Why not? We have a spare room and it's only for a week. Give the girl a break. She's bored and upset. She's away from her family and everything she knows. All she needs is a bit of attention, someone to play with and some love.'

'I think it's an excellent idea,' Mrs Tugg nodded. 'I've been so busy with work. We don't really have the time to give poor Cilla. I'll check with her parents, but I'm sure they'll be more than happy with the new arrangement.'

And that is exactly what has happened. Cilla has moved in. She's bossing me about already – at least she's trying to. She's also taken over training Saucepan and Nibblewibble for the Easter Rabbit Race. I've never seen rabbits run

so fast. (They're probably trying to escape her evil clutches!)

But we've got the chicks sorted out at last. They are amazing and so cuddly! They're going to help us raise loads of money for the new school library. As for Dad, he seems to have gone off chickens.

'I'm going to stick to raising vegetables from now on,' he declared. 'I've had it up to here with newborns.'

'Oh,' said Mum. 'That's a shame.'

'What do you mean?' asked Dad, eyeing her suspiciously.

'Well, Ron, you know those two male rabbits your mother and Lancelot brought us?'

'Yes?'

'It seems that one of them isn't male, after all.'

'What? How do you know?'

'Because Saucepan is pregnant. Soon we shall have a complete set of saucepans. To put it simply, we have baby rabbits on the way.'

Dad closed his eyes and rocked back on his feet with one hand clamped to his head. 'I'm going inside now,' he said quietly. 'I may be some time. I am going to lie down. Please do not disturb me until the world has gone back to being normal.'

And he went indoors. Mum, Cilla and I grinned at each other.

'Well,' smiled Mum. 'Anyone fancy a hot cross bun?'

'Me!' Cilla and I shouted together.

And we marched off to the kitchen, singing.

And I bet you know exactly what we sang!

Ask Jeremy

Of all the books you have written, which one is your favourite?

I loved writing both **KRAZY KOW SAVES THE WORLD – WELL, ALMOST** and **STUFF**, my first book for teenagers. Both these made me laugh out loud while I was writing and I was pleased with the overall result in each case. I also love writing the stories about Nicholas and his daft family – **MY DAD, MY MUM, MY BROTHER** and so on.

If you couldn't be a writer what would you be?

Well, I'd be pretty fed up for a start, because writing was the one thing I knew I wanted to do from the age of nine onward. But if I DID have to do something else, I would love to be either an accomplished pianist or an artist of some sort. Music and art have played a big part in my whole life and I would love to be involved in them in some way.

What's the best thing about writing stories?

Oh dear – so many things to say here! Getting paid for making things up is pretty high on the list! It's also something you do on your own, inside your own head – nobody can interfere with that. The only boss you have is yourself. And you are creating something that nobody else has made before you. I also love making my readers laugh and want to read more and more.

Did you ever have a nightmare teacher? (And who was your best ever?)

My nightmare at primary school was Mrs Chappell, long since dead. I knew her secret – she was not actually human. She was a Tyrannosaurus rex in disguise. She taught me for two years when I was in Y5 and Y6, and we didn't like each other at all. My best ever was when I was in Y3 and Y4. Her name was Miss Cox, and she was the one who first encouraged me to write stories. She was brilliant. Sadly, she is long dead too.

When you were a kid you used to play kiss-chase. Did you always do the chasing or did anyone ever chase you?!

I usually did the chasing, but when I got chased, I didn't bother to run very fast! Maybe I shouldn't admit to that! We didn't play kiss-chase at school – it was usually played during holidays. If we had tried playing it at school we would have been in serious trouble. Mind you, I seemed to spend most of my time in trouble of one sort or another, so maybe it wouldn't have mattered that much.

14½ Things You Didn't Know About

Jeremy Strong

* * * * * * * * * * * * * * * * * * * *

1. He loves eating liquorice.

2. He used to like diving. He once dived from the high board and his trunks came off!

3. He used to play electric violin in a rock band called **THE INEDIBLE CHEESE SANDWICH.**

4. He got a 100-metre swimming certificate when he couldn't even swim.

5. When he was five, he sat on a heater and burnt his bottom.

6. Jeremy used to look after a dog that kept eating his underpants. (No – NOT while he was wearing them!)

7. When he was five, he left a basin tap running with the plug in and flooded the bathroom.

8. He can make his ears waggle.

9. He has visited over a thousand schools.

10. He once scored minus ten in an exam! That's ten less than nothing!

11. His hair has gone grey, but his mind hasn't.

12. He'd like to have a pet tiger.

13. He'd like to learn the piano.

14. He has dreadful handwriting.

And a half . . . His favourite hobby is sleeping. He's very good at it.